Arthur Crawley Chute

John Thomas

First Baptist Missionary to Bengal from 1757 to 1801

Arthur Crawley Chute

John Thomas
First Baptist Missionary to Bengal from 1757 to 1801

ISBN/EAN: 9783337395599

Printed in Europe, USA, Canada, Australia, Japan

Cover: Foto ©Raphael Reischuk / pixelio.de

More available books at **www.hansebooks.com**

JOHN THOMAS,

First Baptist Missionary to Bengal.

1757--1801.

BY

REV. ARTHUR C. CHUTE, B. D.,

PASTOR OF THE FIRST BAPTIST CHURCH, HALIFAX, NOVA SCOTIA.

WITH INTRODUCTION BY

REV. A. J. GORDON, D. D.

"I hope you will always keep some stirring biography on the read. It is most profitable." CATHERINE BOOTH.

HALIFAX, N. S.:
BAPTIST BOOK AND TRACT SOCIETY,
1893.

INTRODUCTION.

We take sincere pleasure in commending the following pages to all students and lovers of Christian Missions. The author of this little biography has put such under real obligation to himself, and he has done a praiseworthy work in lifting out of obscurity a true missionary hero and faithful servant of Jesus Christ.

How often is it the case that a superior man is dwarfed in the shadow of another's greatness, which he himself has helped to create. If William Carey was the pioneer of Modern Missions, John Thomas was the pioneer of Carey. He re'urned from India in that memorable year 1792, to report a work already founded, and to seek assistance for prosecuting it with greater vigor. Thus the Centennial which we have just been keeping marks not only the work of Carey, beginning, but the work of Thomas, begun. And so far as we can see, the great missionary translator and preacher might not have had his face turned towards India, had not the missionary doctor gone before him to prepare the way. It is the story of John the Baptist and

Jesus repeated, with the literal feature accompanying, that as the one increased, the other decreased; Thomas becoming as obscure as Carey became illustrious. Happily the former seems to have had the spirit of the great Forerunner in rejoicing in his eclipse, since he could say: "*Blessed be the Lord, I am safely wrapped up in reproach, while some are exposed to the dangers of fame and reputation.*"

How through poverty and misfortune and ultimate insanity, this good missionary won the above-named beatitude, is admirably told in this compact volume; and the author has done well in seeking that this benediction of obscurity and reproach, so long worn, shall at last be crowned with a worthy benediction of honor and appreciation. The substance and the style of Mr. Chute's missionary monograph, its literary finish and its historical fulness, merit for it a place in permanent missionary biography. Such honor the writer of this introduction cordially bespeaks for it.

A. J. GORDON.

Boston, November 10th, 1893.

PREFACE.

Why should a monograph on John Thomas be written? And why should it be read? A three-fold answer may be given. In the *first* place, Thomas was a brave pioneer in the modern Missionary Movement. He was the first to preach to the Bengalese in their own language, having preceded William Carey some years. By him the Society formed at Kettering (1792) was led to begin its operations in India. From him Carey received his first instructions in Bengali. It was he who first began to translate the Bible into the Bengali tongue; and through his preaching, Krishna Pal, the first heathen convert of the Serampore Mission, was won. In the *second* place, the defects and eccentricities of his life and character are more generally known than his many good qualities and the profit of his ministry. There was much in his career well suited to quicken faith and beget heroic endeavor on the part of those who toil upon trying fields. In the *third* place, his biography, as written by Rev. C. B. Lewis, is not only large and closely-packed, but is now out of print and hardly obtainable. For these reasons, therefore, there is need of a brochure on Thomas among our missionary booklets; and it is hoped the following pages may in some measure meet the demand.

By the courtesy of Mr. Edward Goodman, of the Chicago *Standard*, there appear cuts of Thomas, Carey and Fuller, and of that building of historic interest—the home of Mrs. Wallis at Kettering.

A. C. CHUTE.

Halifax, Nova Scotia,
   October 12th, 1893.

CONTENTS.

"And Jesus came and spake unto them, saying: All power is given unto me in heaven and in earth. Go ye therefore, and teach all nations, baptizing them in the name of the Father, and of the Son, and of the Holy Ghost: teaching them to observe all things whatsoever I have commanded you: and, lo, I am with you alway even unto the end of the world. Amen."

—MAT. 28: 18–20.

JOHN THOMAS.

CHAPTER I.

BOTH SIDES.

" Most people help those who do not need it; every traveller throws a stone where there is a heap already; all cooks baste the fat pig, and the lean one gets burned."
—C. H. SPURGEON.

In the biographies of William Carey there is just enough said of John Thomas to make the reader curious to know more. And most of what is said does not give a very favorable impression of him. Those who have not carefully looked into his life-story may think of him as little more than an imprudent, debt-contracting man who hindered the cause of Missions rather more than he helped it. Indeed, so widely prevalent is this notion that one cannot well ignore it in giving a sketch of his life. Writers upon Carey's work desire to pay that wonderful "little man with a far-off look" every possible honor; and it may happen sometimes that Thomas is unintentionally made to suffer in order to add to the glory of the greater man. But Carey has need of no glory other than what comes of an accurate recital of his achievements, while Thomas assuredly has need that justice be done him.   The defects in the character and life of the latter have been extensively advertized ; while his excellencies, which were many and marked, have had little publicity.   It will certainly not be amiss, then, while the labors of " the consecrated cobbler" are still under full review, in connection with the Centenary of Modern Missions, to recount also the deeds of the consecrated surgeon, as far as these had to do with the planting of Christianity in the Indian Empire.

Thomas had peculiar trials to encounter.   He had much in his constitution to contend with ; and outside there were grievous difficulties against which he had to fight stoutly to the end.   But, notwithstanding all that was adverse, he wrought for the divine Master in a manner that cannot fail to command in many ways our admiration, and the gratitude of the Christian world.   He helped, more than is generally recognized, in paving the way for the success which attended the devoted and varied labors of the famous trio at Serampore—Carey, Marshman and Ward.

Any who have not closely followed his career, and would like to do so, are recommended to procure, if they can, his biography as written by Rev. C. B. Lewis (London: Macmillan and Co., 1873), an octavo of more than four hundred pages. The book is somewhat monotonous and unentertaining, it is true, but the reader will come upon much therein that is of worth concerning early attempts to win India for Christ; and as he reads on through copious extracts from the journal of Dr. Thomas, he will find his heart going out with tenderness toward the much afflicted and often downcast, while always nobly heroic, missionary whose story it seeks to unfold. Sometimes the tear will start from the eye at beholding the complicated troubles through which the good man ever strove to make his onward way.

If it be said that a missionary making so defective a history had as well not be written about, our answer is that the failings which attach to men are often as instructive as their virtues. In fact, it is through the agency of imperfect men and women, and no others, for others there are none, that God is winning the world unto Himself. "The most careful driver," says John Ploughman, "one day upsets the cart, the cleverest cook spills a little broth, and as I know to my sorrow, a very decent ploughman will now and then break the plough and often make a crooked furrow."

CHAPTER II.

A GLANCE AT INDIA.

"The prejudices and persecutions of heathens were a sore enough trial, but sorer and more hopeless was the wicked and contaminating influence of, alas, my fellow-countrymen."—JOHN G. PATON.

"When graceless white men go away from all the restraints of society, from public opinion, from the salt of the earth, from the indirect influences of Christianity, they seem to become demons."—HENRY RICHARDS.

It will help us first of all to take a glance at Calcutta as it was prior to the time Thomas came there.

After the Black Hole tragedy, when about a hundred and fifty Englishmen were cruelly suffocated in that city (June 20, 1756), Lord Clive won a victory for England on the plain of Plassey (June 23, 1757)—a victory which was the beginning of the empire of Britain in the East. Just when England was, by her own injustice and colonial resentment, relaxing her grasp upon the American colonies, she was laying firm hold upon Eastern possessions. While America could get along better without her domination, India had need that she should obtain there such power as would eventually turn out to the furtherance of the gospel amongst the millions of idolators. And though many influential Englishmen were at first foes of Indian missionaries, the day came when those who sought the salvation of the heathen in that country had government support in their work of love.

The British East India Company, at first nothing more than a commercial organization, but afterwards a recognized branch of the English government, was bent solely upon financial gain. Therefore it toadied to heathen customs and would not permit interference with Brahmanism. There was not amongst most of those connected with it enough of Christianity to make them at all desirous that a false religion should give place to the true.

Some little provision of a religious nature was made for the Company's servants in India. A church had been erected in 1715 in Calcutta, while the Company was simply commercial; but this was destroyed at the time of the Black Hole horror. The year after his great triumph, Clive invited Kiernander, a Swede, mainly from personal and political motives, to come from Tranquebar, on the Coromandel coast (where Frederick IV., of Denmark, had sent Zeigenbalg and Plutschau in 1705—a mission which received aid from the English "Society for Promoting Christian Knowledge") for the purpose of establishing a mission in Calcutta. Kiernander came; and he continued his labors there until 1787, about three years after Thomas first visited Bengal. But no great results, at least of a sort clearly traceable, issued from his ministry. Kiernander knew not the language of the heathen, so that his work was confined to Europeans. In Calcutta he built a church, largely at his own expense, having become rich by a second marriage. That public morals were low, there and then, is indicated by the fact that his friends claimed for him much credit because he did not permit the brick-layers to work upon the edifice on Sunday. Though Kiernander was a benevolent man, it does not appear that he greatly gloried in the Cross of Jesus Christ. In his seventy-sixth year he was overtaken by financial ruin; and when it was thought to dispose of his mission church for an auction room, Charles Grant, a distinguished servant of the East India Company, and an earnest Christian, purchased the building that it might continue to be used for divine worship. Here, for more than twenty years, beginning April 6, 1787, Rev. David Brown, of the Church of England, who came

to India a month before Thomas, to take charge
of the Orphan House at Howrah, preached to
a small audience of his own countrymen. All
the while there prevailed among Englishmen in
Bengal, duelling and deism, drunkenness and
gambling. In social life there was extreme
depravity. What was presented in the lives of
English residents was not calculated to give the
heathen a favorable idea of Christianity. As a
rule the servants of the Company, freed from
the restraints of Christian society at home, gave
loose rein to the baser propensities. As Steven-
son says in his *Dawn of the Modern Mission:*
" These settlements from Christian countries
had no direct influence on the Christianizing of
India, unless it were an influence for evil. They
were long a scandal and a stumbling-block in
the way of missionary effort."

But amidst the godless Englishmen of India
there were godly exceptions. Among these few
was the Evangelical Churchman just referred
to, Charles Grant. In 1767 he went East in
the military service and was soon promoted to
responsible positions. Through domestic afflic-
tions he was led to seek the consolations of the
gospel ; and from that on was anxious, not only
for the spiritual welfare of the Europeans who
were in India, but for the vast heathen popula-

tion of that dark land. Therefore he, along
with his pious brother-in-law, William Chambers,
drew up proposals for the establishment of a
Protestant mission in Bengal and Behar. These
were submitted to such evangelicals at home as
John Newton, Thomas Scott, Charles Simeon
and William Wilberforce. Grant said that he
would himself pay the salaries of two missionaries until a public fund could be established
for their support ; but he believed that little or
nothing could be accomplished until government sanction were secured   It was emphati-
cally declared that " *In every mission scheme
for Bengal, the protection of government is
indispensably requisite.*" Visiting England, he
earnestly sought to obtain this protection ; and
when the charter of the Company came to be
renewed (1793) attempts were made, but in
vain, to introduce clauses providing for the
spread of Christianity among Indian peoples.
About this time, however, there originated in
Northamptonshire, among a few humble Non-
conformist ministers, a movement destined to
succeed without government patronage and in
spite of its opposition.

CHAPTER III.

THE WAYWARD YOUTH AND THE SURGEON OF AN INDIAMAN.

"As the sea was returned to its smoothness of surface and settled calmness by the abatement of that storm, so the hurry of my thoughts being over, my fears and apprehensions of being swallowed up by the sea being forgotten, and the current of my former desires returned, I entirely forgot the vows and promises that I made in my distress."
—ROBINSON CRUSOE.

There is no full information regarding the early life of John Thomas.

He was born in the town of Fairford, Gloucestershire, England, May 16, 1757, a little more than four years before the birth of Carey in Northamptonshire. When in his eleventh year he lost his mother. His father was a godly deacon of the Baptist Church in the town; and to the deacon's house neighboring ministers often came, of whom special mention may be made of Benjamin Beddome, the hymn writer.

From early years this son was ambitious to be a preacher; but not quickly did he yield himself to a godly life. There were seasons now and again when he was under deep conviction of sin, but radical renewal was delayed. "We may start out of our common course, when

shook, like the needle of a compass," he himself once said; "but, the disturbance over, we
turn to our track again."

Jack, as he was called, was not noted in
youth for steadiness. Though having excellent
abilities he did not distinguish himself at school,
for he much preferred out-door sports to books.
Several attempts were made to put him to an
apprenticeship, but he would not keep at that
to which he was set. At length, being sent to
Westminster Hospital, he found in medical
study something congenial, and so made good
progress therein. As soon as necessary qualifications were secured he was appointed assistant
surgeon on one of His Majesty's ships.

Once when out to sea, the ship sprang a leak
and the situation was perilous. But, as he afterwards wrote, "that immeasurable goodness, that
unsearchable Providence which so often ban-
ishes our terrors and fears, though ever so
violent, adapted our relief to the measure of our
distress so nicely, that we did not let go our
hope till it was swallowed up in the enjoyment
of a safe arrival in harbor. This affecting preservation from death," he adds, "changed my
opinions on religious matters, which otherwise
had about this time been strongly biased by
principles of rank infidelity and deism." Not yet,

however, did he make surrender of his heart
to God   When the wind veered and he was
safe in port, the goodness of the heavenly
Father was put from his remembrance. Crusoe-
like, "I hardened in harbor into my old sins
and forgot the God of my mercies."

Leaving the Navy he opened business in London as surgeon and apothecary ; and then, at
twenty-four, took to himself a Church of England girl to wife, although, as he tells us, he
would have preferred to have had her a Baptist. The references to her in his biography
are few and incidental, but those that appear
advance her in an agreeable light.   After marriage he now and then attended places of
worship, a custom he seems to have abandoned
for a season ; and one day he was so wrought
upon by a sermon he heard that, like many
another before and since, he went about to
effect outward reform.   A little later, hearing
Dr. Stennett and turning eagerly to the Scriptures, he accepted Christ as his Saviour.   "And
then, " he says, "my assurance of pardon and
everlasting happiness ran high and strong, without any intermission, for a long time "

It was at this period in the life of Thomas,
we may notice, that Lord Cornwallis was com-

pelled to surrender to Washington at Yorktown,
Virginia (Oct. 19, 1781).

But the "long time" of which he speaks was
only about four months. He was quite a man
for the hill top, but not for abiding there long
together. Having too sanguine expectations of
financial prosperity he entered into debt, and so
into trouble and perplexity. Then unexpect-
edly there came to him one day a way of relief
in the offer of the surgeoncy of a ship bound
to the East Indies. This position he gladly
accepted and went on board the *Earl of Oxford*
early in 1783—the year Carey was baptized by
the younger Ryland. Not yet, however, had
he made public profession of religion, some
friends restraining him on account of past un-
steadiness. During the voyage he won a good
name as a physician, and was therefore asked on
his return, September, 1784, to take a second
voyage. The ensuing Christmas day he was
baptized by Rev. Mr. Burnham; and as the ship
was not sent out in 1785, he was employed
until she sailed with preaching in town and
country.

Within the year 1785 the subject of our
sketch was powerfully impressed by the perusal
of Isaiah forty-ninth, and he thought the Lord
then called him to go afar and preach to the

Gentiles. There was awakened in him the hope, which he cherished even in the gloomiest times which succeeded, that God would through him do much for the heathen. " I understood that the Lord would surprise me with numbers surpassing my crediting powers : that I should stand astonished at it ; and that great personages should be among those who would nurse and take care of me and mine, and the temporal affairs of the Lord's sheep." But his large expectations he never saw fulfilled. Nevertheless, he toiled on bravely to the end with such confidence in God as we do not often see surpassed.

CHAPTER IV.

JOHN THOMAS AND CHARLES GRANT.

"The contention was so sharp between them, that they departed asunder one from the other."—Acts 15 : 39.

"The regenerate and the unregenerate differ in their motives and their ends; the one party are governed by regard to this world, the other by regard to eternity; but the differences of good men respect only minor arrangements for promoting the benefit of mankind and the glory of God."—ROBERT HALL.

In March of 1786, Dr. Thomas again sailed for India. On reaching there he was introduced to the little circle of Christians then in Calcutta, and was warmly welcomed. Strongly desirous of seeing India won for Christ, Charles Grant expressed the wish that Thomas, who was fervently devoted to Christian work, might remain in Bengal and preach the gospel to the heathen.

This proposal, as will be seen, was entirely in accord with the aspirations begotten in the Christian surgeon by that chapter in Isaiah. But there were obstacles in the way of acceding to Grant's desire. Behind him in England the doctor had left his family, and before him in India was the task of acquiring a difficult language. Furthermore, he was already employed

as a ship's officer, and how could he allow the
ship to return without him ? But these things
were surmountable. As for his family, they
could come later, and by dint of diligence the
new tongue could be mastered. But what about
his position on ship board ? Between him and
fellow officers some unpleasantness had arisen
because he had been so taken up with religious
matters on shore ; and on account of this variance
Thomas was the more anxious to get free from
the engagement which bound him. The night
of Jan. 12, 1787, was spent by him in medita-
tion and prayer, and the conclusion was reached
that God would have him stay and begin work
with a view to saving the benighted pagans.
Accordingly, after quite a financial surrender,
his connection with the ship was severed.

Engaging a moonshee of the writer caste,
Ram Basu by name, afterwards Carey's teacher,
he earnestly set about to learn Bengali, the
language of the common people. But besides
this he must also labor the while for the
spiritual welfare of European residents. At
the outset of the new effort it seemed that
everything would move smoothly. Thomas
soon found it to be one thing, however, to be
engaged in Christian service during times of
leisure from the ship, and quite another, and

more difficult thing, to be regularly employed
as a religious instructor. Grant, occupying a
prominent official position, mingled much more
with the world than Thomas regarded as
proper ; and the newly-engaged missionary
wrote in his journal : " Reputation is a snare to
those who are called to follow Him who made
Him elf of no reputation." This was the com-
mencement of failing sympathy between these
two worthy men.

Rev. David Brown, of whom mention has
been made, was not among those who had to do
with enlisting Thomas in this enterprise.   Had
he been consulted it is probable he would have
pointed out difficulties likely to arise between a
Baptist missionary and Pædobaptist supporters.
Brown and Thomas were men of totally differ-
ent make-up, and they could not well get along
together.   As a preacher Brown was scholarly
and unattractive, though quite evangelical ;
while Thomas was vivacious and popular, and
evangelical to a high degree.   Thomas hoped
Grant would make him minister at Kiernander's mission church until he had acquired the
Bengali tongue ; but in this he was disapointed,
for Brown was chosen to the office.

Grant now desired Thomas to go up country
three hundred miles to Malda, where one of the

Udny brothers lived, and there study the vernacular and preach to Europeans ; and then
later, when Bengali had been learned, to remove
to Goamalty, near by, where Grant owned a
tract of land and an indigo factory. Into this
plan Thomas entered, May, 1787, although he
would greatly have preferred remaining where
he was until he could preach to the natives.
His brief labors in Calcutta had resulted in the
conversion of two or three young Englishmen,
one of whom, Robert Thomas Burney, was the
means of turning many to Christ within the
twenty years of subsequent continuance there.

Before going north the missionary made in his
diary an entry which may here be quoted as
representing the place given in his life to prayer
and the study of the Scriptures. It indicates,
too, his desires and expectations with respect to
those sitting in darkness. " Day and night,"
he says, " I meditate on the word of God and
have much fellowship with Him, and much confidence of being sent with a message from God
to these poor heathens, and that the Lord will
certainly bless the preaching of the gospel now
at this very time. I have said that the gospel
would never depart from this country till the
glory of the latter times comes. I have made
my boast of God amongst the people, and told

them that I had unshaken trust in God ; and I
do not think of being ashamed of this boasting ;
but believe what God hath spoken concerning
those that wait for Him and put their trust in
Him. . . O for a seeking *first* His kingdom
daily ! O for the marrow of His word, the energy
of His Spirit, and the sober consolations of unin-
terrupted fellowship with Him. But I do not
desire consolations only, seeing it is best sometimes to suffer ; therefore I throw the reins to
Jesus, not with an air of carnal ease, but with
the utmost desire that He should undertake the
work of guiding and governing me through a
slippery, dangerous path."

On the 18th of June, 1787, he reached
Malda, where he was cordially received into
the home of George Udny, brother of Robert,
one of the circle of Christians in Calcutta.
But Thomas took away with him overmuch
care of the brethren he left behind. William
Chambers and others were harboring Armin-
ianism — a thing that Calvinistic Thomas
could ill brook. He wished that at the beginning of the gospel stream in Bengal there might
be purity ; but his method of seeking to secure
it did not work to advantage. At great length
he wrote to correct what he thought serious
error—wrote in quite a dogmatic and dictatorial

way. Of the displeasure produced thereby Grant was a partaker. In the first letter written by Carey to the Society that afterwards sent him and Thomas forth as their first missionaries, Carey has this to say of his colleague : " The more I know, the more I love him. He is a very holy man—but his faithfulness often degenerates into personality, which may account for the difference between Mr. Grant and him."*

When Thomas saw that by his plain correspondence, at the time of which we are speaking, serious offence had been given, he wrote with exceeding tenderness to Chambers, for he was not a man whose eyes never became opened to his mistakes, nor was it little that he grieved over them when he saw them. One sentence from this epistle we may here give as suitable

---

*See *Serampore Letters*, edited by Leighton and Mornay Williams. G. P. Putnam's Sons, New York and London, 1892. An exceedingly interesting book.—In reading the letter from which the above is taken—all the letters of the volume appearing just as they were written—one is reminded of what Fuller once wrote Carey. The missionary had asked the secretary to adhere, when publishing what he wrote, to his mode of spelling Indian words, whereupon Fuller made the following rejoinder: "But you do not always spell alike. Sometimes you write *moonshee*, and sometimes *munshi*. 'If the trumpet give an uncertain sound, who can prepare for the battle?' You must again allow me to remind you of your *punctuation*. I never knew a person of so much knowledge as you possess of other languages, write English so bad! You huddle half-a-dozen periods into one. Where your sentence ends, you very commonly make only a semicolon, instead of a period. If your Bengali New Testament should be thus pointed, I should tremble for its fate."

to be remembered in connection with his own pioneer missionary labor as a whole : "You are sensible," he says, "that I meant to do you good, and not evil, in what is past, and also that young beginners do mischief before they do good, in most trades and callings, and sometimes it is the same in the gospel." We may add that but for the mistakes of predecessors, there would be less of success to successors. But to God be all the glory !

The ill feeling between Grant and Thomas kept increasing. After the latter had been about two months in Malda, his mind was turned to the neglect of the Lord's Supper in which the little band of Christians there was living, and he determined that the ordinance should be administered once a month. First of all, however, he thought he ought to insist on the immersion of all who desired to participate. Accordingly, he began to speak out plainly upon the subject of baptism, and also to communicate with the Calcutta friends about it. "If the tiny pins of a watch," he wrote, "are of so much value and use, notwithstanding their smallness, and if it be essential that they are rightly placed, who can say that the ordinances of God's house are less so?" Convinced of the importance of the matter, he prepared a

pamphlet against infant sprinkling and in
support of believer's baptism. This he supposed
would silence all objectors and at once bring
them over to his view, for he had not yet
learned that " nothing is so hopelessly obstinate
as theological traditional prejudice."

This controversy caused the Pædobaptist
friends of the man who was always loyal to
truth, as he understood it, cost what it might,
to draw off from him. To counteract his influence, if possible, books were sent up from
Calcutta to Malda. But in spite of this, one
man, William Long, who belonged to the
civilian circle in which Thomas moved, became
satisfied that the Baptist position was Scriptural,
and was baptized, June 13, 1788, probably the
first administration of Bible baptism ever
occurring in Bengal. When the report of the
event came south, Robert Udny wrote Thomas
questioning the authority of a layman to bap-
tize. " I wonder," says Thomas, " what he
thinks ' a minister ' to be! I have been
ministering to him these twelve months, and
yet he is unwilling to allow me the same
authority as a poor uncalled, unsent, uncon-
verted, but ordained gownsman!" At this
point the humble Baptist missionary was in
collision with a great ecclesiastical system ; but
he had the right of it, nevertheless.

Moreover, Thomas was now in a financial strait. His release from the ship had cost him considerable, and for Indian muslins sent to the English market he had received scarcely half what was reckoned upon. Besides, Grant's waning friendship made his income from that source precarious. In his extremity, George Udny, who was perhaps as faithful a friend as he ever had, although much affected by the attitude of Grant, offered to advance Thomas half of what he then required, provided Grant would advance the other half. This Grant was not inclined to do; but after a while he agreed to the proposal upon certain conditions. Thomas must remove to Goamalty, near the ruins of the ancient city of Gour, must cease troubling Malda and Calcutta with his Baptist notions, and must not publish the translation of Matthew which he had just completed. The reason why printing of the translation was opposed is not quite evident. Perhaps Grant did not have confidence in the excellence of the work, and he may have been reserving his support for the translation which his brother-in-law, Chambers, contemplated making, but never made.

But Thomas will receive help upon no such terms as those stated, great as is his need of money. He will remain a loyal Baptist, and will do his utmost to have the gospel of Matthew speedily published. And very soon, therefore, the breach between Grant and Thomas is made complete. But just before the final separation, Grant gave 500 rupees (nearly $250) and George Udny as much more, to build for Thomas a bungalow at Harla Gachi, six miles from Udny's residence, which the missionary began to occupy in October of 1789. Then on the 7th of the following month, Grant informed Thomas by letter that henceforth he would cut off all allowances from him, and advised him to return to the practice of medicine. George Udny likewise declined further assistance for a while.

It was about this time, we may recall in passing, that Thomas first witnessed the burning of a widow upon the pyre of the dead husband. The year 1829 was a memorable one for India, because then, largely through Carey's efforts, this inhuman practice of Suttee was abolished by law. But ten years before Carey saw a case of this sort, Thomas looked upon it, August 30, 1789, and began immediately to exert himself to bring the horrible thing to an end. An account cf this first scene he published in two Calcutta papers of September 3, 1789, the *Gazette* and *Chronicle*; and urged the duty

of government interference with this heathen
custom.

In connection with the above-mentioned
withdrawal of temporal aid, it has been custom-
ary to lay the blame upon Thomas. But it is
worth while to recall what Carey wrote in 1796
touching the affair. This is what he says:
" Mr. Grant's opposition to the work, I think
abominable. The fact is, as can be proved by a
long correspondence between him and Mr.
Thomas, now in preservation, that Mr. Thomas
left a much more lucrative employment and the
society of his family, at Mr. Grant's desire, to
preach the gospel among the natives; who
afterwards, because he would not conform to
his peremptory dictates, in matters which he
could not conscienticusly do, cut off all his
supplies and left him to shift for himself in a
foreign land."

And listen to Thomas's own words at this
trying time: " I am afar off from riches, reputation and worldly pleasures. Many are they
who rise up against me. Some are displeased
with me for preaching at all; others are displeased with me for preaching to the natives.
Others threaten me if I should print my translation. Others are angry because I preach the
baptism of Christ and His apostles. Others,

that I will not administer the bread and wine
to them, because they were never rightly baptized. Others are angry with me for personal
reproof, etc. But the greatest question of all
is, whether *He* be angry or no, in whose name
I continue to say and to teach these things....
My wife and family not coming out, is a grief
to me. My circumstances are another source
of trouble ; but I believe that, by my poverty,
the Lord is trying those who are rich and able,
and on whom it is very incumbent to relieve
me ; and in due time I hope to be relieved.
But, if not, I had rather be as I am than as
they are ; and blessed be God always, that He
has afflicted and tried me, and, by some indis-
cretion of my own, brought me into a state of
poverty and dependence. Blessed be the Lord,
I am more safely wrapped up in reproach, while
some are exposed to the dangers of fame and
reputation." He continues : "I begin to get
old and this country will quicken my pace. It
cannot be much longer ; 1 may safely begin to
take leave. Adieu, vain and empty world, vile
and sinful body, frail and fluttering friends,
kind and sterling brethren! Adieu. But where
I am going must be considered, and alas, I can
not well say. I cannot truly constantly think,
I am betwixt two opinions of myself. I have

too much hatred of sin, and too much love for
that which is good, to think myself still in the
bonds of iniquity; and I have too many of
those things which grow on corrupt trees to
think steadily that I am a child of God. Sometimes I find my hopes are beyond all painful
scruples; but never find my despair and doubt
beyond any comfortable hope."

Poor lonely man! Multiform and heavy
were thy hardships. But through grace thou
didst triumph; and so may we. Difficulties are
leaden steps upon which we may go up to a
golden throne.

THE HOME OF MRS. WALLIS, AT KETTERING.

CHAPTER V.

THE BACK PARLOR.

"How far that little candle throws his beams!"
—SHAKSPEARE.

"If my hand slacked,
I should rob God, since He is fullest good,
Leaving a blank instead of violins.
He could not make Antonio Stradivari's violins
Without Antonio."—GEORGE ELIOT.

At Harla Gachi, where the bungalow had been erected, Thomas went on, as best he could, with his translation and mission work, though sometimes much put about to secure the necessaries of life. Once when he was ready to give up his boat, or anything he had, to a creditor, the goodwill of George Udny was shown in discharging the debt.

In the middle of 1790, there appeared encouraging signs in the work among the natives, so that the Malda friends agreed to allow him a monthly stipend. But a larger and more certain means of support was required. Therefore Thomas began to contemplate a return to England to stir up an interest there in his labors; and more and more, as the year 1791 advanced, did he become assured that this should be the next step.   He had no thought whatever, sorely as he had been tried, of abandoning the missionary undertaking.   His purpose in coming home is thus stated in a letter to his brother :— " You need not be surprised to see me in England, perhaps about the middle of 1792 ; for I intend to take my passage this season. My intention is to make types, procure a press, also a fellow-laborer ; and, if I can, establish a fund in London for the support of this work, and also to regain my family, and return after eight months' stay in England."

The latter part of 1791 was spent by him at Nuddea, the Hindoo Oxford, where he studied Sanscrit, the language in which the Hindoo sacred books are written, with Padma Lochan as his tutor, and enjoyed much kindness at the hands of the learned Sir William Jones.

On the 30th of January, 1792, *annus mirabilis*, he left Calcutta for his native country ; and on the ninth of July following, was with his family in England, having been separated from them for the space of six years and four months.

Leaving Thomas for a little, let us now attend to some events which led up to a friendly reception for him in the home land.

At this period there existed among Christian people in general utter indifference to the condition of the heathen world, although there were already several soc'eties which were attempting something in foreign mission work. But now there came a real waking up, on the part of a few persons, to the duty of the whole Church of God in the matter of gospel extension ; and these few were so faith-filled and persistent that they could not rest until a society for sending the glad tidings of great joy into distant parts was formed upon a much broader and firmer basis, and with larger designs, than ever yet known.

Towards that missionary awakening there were three treatises in particular that contributed much. The first was by Jonathan Edwards of New England. In 1744 a few Scottish ministers banded together to pray especially for the spread of the gospel in the world ; and two years later they communicated with the Christians of North America asking them to join in this exercise. Thereupon Edwards wrote his " Humble attempt to promote explicit agreement and visible union of God's people in extraordinary prayer for the revival of religion and the advancement of Christ's kingdom on earth." This, mainly through the efforts of John Sutcliff, Baptist pastor at Olney, was reprinted and circulated in England ; and its influence was so great in the Northamptonshire Baptist Association that the pastors composing that body formed, in 1784, the "monthly concert" for prayer.

The second treatise was by "the Franklin of theology," Andrew Fuller, a man who was, under God, a mighty power in the historical epoch under review. By him the churches were aroused to meet their financial obligations to those afar off, and the English government was wrought upon to grant missionaries of the Cross liberty to go to India and preach and teach (1813). Those who have read Dr. John Brown's touching story of *Rab and his Friends*, will remember the reference there to Fuller. "You must have observed," the writer says, "the likeness of certain men to certain animals, and of certain dogs to men. Now, I never looked at Rab without thinking of the great Baptist preacher, Andrew Fuller. The same large, heavy, menacing, combative, sombre, honest countenance, the same deep inevitable eye, the same look—as of thunder asleep, but ready—neither a dog nor a man to be trifled with."

But to return to the second tractate. It bore the title, " The Gospel Worthy of all Acceptation," and made its appearance the year after the "monthly concert" was established. This struck a telling blow at the prevailing hyper-Calvinism which held men back from any aggressive effort in the way of seeking the salvation of the unregenerate.

The third treatise, and the most remarkable one, was by William Carey. While Thomas was toiling in and about Malda, ambitious to do something to win heathen India for Christ, Carey, the shoemaker-preacher of Moulton and Leicester, was having his eyes opened to the needs of the heathen world on the one hand and to the import of the Great Commission on the other. The result of his studies and prayers was embodied in his " Enquiry into the Obligations of Christians to use Means for the conversion of the Heathens." For some time the piece was laid by in manuscript, for the author had no money with which to print it. But one day, meeting in Birmingham deacon Thomas Potts, of Pearce's Church, the deacon wanted to know of him what it was he had in his head about missions ; and when he learned of what Carey had written, and the cause of its being kept from the public, he furnished ten pounds with which to publish it, and the treatise was soon abroad doing effective work. It appeared at Leicester in 1792.

Besides these three treatises, there were also three sermons, preached in the Association afore-mentioned, that had much influence. Two of them were delivered in 1791 at Clipstone—one by Sutcliff and the other by Fuller. They were both discourses which deepened the conviction of the hearers that guilt rested upon the Church of God in not carrying the good news to distant and benighted peoples. The other was Carey's noted sermon, given at Nottingham, May 31, 1792, while Thomas was homeward bound, from Isaiah 54 : 2, 3, with the memorable divisions : " Expect great things from God," and "Attempt great things for God." After this was delivered, Carey called for some immediate action, for none were so eager for prompt and definite effort as he ; and it was at once agreed that by the next ministers' meeting, in the ensuing October, a plan should be presented at Ketter-ing, where Fuller had his pastorate, for organ-izing a foreign missionary society.

Accordingly, on the evening of the 2nd of October, 1792, in the back parlor of the house of Mrs. Beeby Wallis,* widow of a departed

* The house still stands and is visible from the Midland Railway.

deacon of Fuller's church, there was formed
what received the name of "The Particular
Baptist Missionary Society for Propagating the
Gospel amongst the Heathen."

It must not be forgotten that there were
foreign missionary societies before this, and
care must needs be taken, especially by Baptists,
lest the work done by these be underrated. But
it may be justly affirmed that their purposes and
achievements were comparatively feeble and
limited. As is said in the introduction to *A
Handbook of Foreign Missions* (1888): "The
revival of the true apostolic ideal, of going to a
people on the evangelical errand, neither as con-
queror nor as colonist, and of winning the
nations for Christ without interfering with their
independence or asserting any kind of authority
over them, was a result of the great revival of
religion in England during the latter part of the
eighteenth century; and among the foremost
pioneers of the work was William Carey." Or
again, in the utterance of Dr. Murdock, found
in his admirable address* delivered at the
Centenary in Philadelphia (1892): "One of the
aspects which differentiated the new era from
every movement which had preceded it, was

---

* *A Century of Missions and its Lessons*, by Rev. J.
N. Murdock, D. D.

that it organized the home work of missions in
a way to give unity to missionary counsels and
permanence to missionary efforts. The work of
others had failed because it had no basis of
direction and supply in the home churches.
The earlier missions were personal and not
organic. They were, indeed, fruits of the best
spiritual fervors of the Reformation, but they
had no roots in the churches of the Reformation."

But now that the first Baptist Society had
been formed, serious questions confronted its
officers. Who will go as missionaries? Where
are funds to be had with which to send them?
And to what part of the world ought they to
turn? For one, Carey was ready to depart as
a missionary for any quarter of the globe. As
to funds, Carey and Fuller were prepared to
enter upon the work of soliciting contributions.
As to a field, Carey thought of Tahiti, in the
South Seas, or Western Africa; while his friend
Samuel Pearce was inclined to propose the
Pelew Islands. Fifty years later than this,
David Livingstone had an eye on China, but
the Lord, through Robert Moffat, who was
visiting home, directed him to South Africa.
And now, through John Thomas, the great
Head of the Church drew the attention of the
newly-formed Society to India. A little boy

named John Williams, afterwards an iron-
monger's apprentice, was being prepared of God
for the South Seas, and the "London Missionary Society" was soon born to send him.

Three months before that parlor meeting,
Thomas reached his native land and began
forthwith to arouse interest in his worthy aims.
Dr. Gordon has said, in speaking of the opening
up of Africa by David Livingstone on the one
hand, and the simultaneous abolition of American slavery by Abraham Lincoln on the other,
that God never makes half a providence any
more than man makes half a pair of shears.
To cite another illustration of the truth thus
strikingly put, recall the remarkable work of
William Carey and his associates in making
many translations of the Scriptures, beginning
with the Bengali. In that is seen one half of
another providence. And here is the other half :
Mary Jones, a Welsh peasant girl, carefully
puts by for six years her little earnings with
which to buy a Bible, and when the required
sum is gathered, walks barefooted twenty-
five miles from her home to make the purchase.
Seeing her grief at learning that one could not
be had, because all were promised, Thomas
Charles was so moved that he sent her away
with the coveted treasure. Then Charles

raised the cry, " We must have a society for distributing Bibles through Wales," a cry which expanded upon the lips of Joseph Hughes into the exclamation : " If for Wales, why not for the world ?" And thus originated the " British and Foreign Bible Society " (1804) for the circulation of God's Word in every tongue.*

Now in the missionary uprising in England, and in the home-coming of Dr. Thomas at this juncture, there was completeness. As Lewis remarks : " But for Thomas, it is to the last degree unlikely that this Society would have thought seriously of India as their field of labor. But for the Society, it is more than probable that Thomas would have failed to evoke the sympathy and support essential to the continuance of his work."

To Thomas the attention of the Committee was immediately turned. Of his efforts among the Hindoos they were not entirely ignorant. He had corresponded with Stennett, Booth and the elder Ryland, and there was already some interest in his labors. Fuller, the Secretary, was appointed by the Society to make inquiry concerning his " character, principles, ability

---

*For an interesting account of this, see the little volume: *The Story of Mary Jones and her Bible.* London: British and Foreign Bible Society ; and also an article by Dr. Farrar in *Review of the Churches,* January 15th, 1892.

and success "; and the investigation left a
favorable impression. The correspondence of
Thomas with the home brethren was examined;
and the difficulties between him and Grant were
looked into. " We read," says Fuller, " the
letters which had passed between Mr. Thomas
and a very respectable gentleman who had employed him in India. It seemed to us that he
had been rather too warm ; yet this difference
did not sink him, in any considerable degree, in
our estimation."

It is worth noting that it was at this very
time that Charles Grant was in England
trying to carry out his scheme for India's
spiritual welfare, having left the East nearly
two years before Thomas, or just after he with-
drew from Thomas the support he had been
giving him.

As the outcome of investigation and conference, Thomas and Carey were accepted as missionaries to India, and the two, with Fuller,
went about collecting the money needed above
what had already come in. Nor was this an easy
task. The main body of the Christian people were
not at all in sympathy with the enterprise, while
some were decidedly opposed to it. London ministers, with the exception of John Newton, stood
aloof. Even Dr. Stennett counseled his metro-

politan brethren "not to commit themselves."
But the movement was of God and could not be
stayed.

On the 20th of March, 1793, the Society
solemnly set apart at Leicester, the modern
Antioch, their Barnabas and Saul for the work
whereunto the Holy Ghost had called them;
and shortly John Thomas and William Carey
were on the way to their assigned field.

This new venture, let us notice, brought
marvelous gain to the country where it had
origin; for apathy at home needed smiting as
well as heathenism abroad. What Fuller re-
marked of himself might with equal truth be
spoken of his own and other religious bodies.
"Before this," he said, "I did little but pine
over my misery, but since I have betaken myself to greater activity for God, my strength has
been recovered, and my soul relpenished." Or,
as he elsewhere wrote: "We consider the
mission to Bengal as the most favorable
symptom attending our denomination. It
confirms what has been for some time with me
an important principle, that where any denomination, congregation, (or individual) seeks only
its own, it will be disappointed, but where it
seeks the kingdom of God and His righteousness, its own prosperity will be among the

things that will be added unto it." "Then the shepherds," runs the Dream of the Tinker, "took Christiana and her company and had them to Mount Charity, where they showed them a man that had a bundle of cloth lying before him, out of which he cut coats and garments for the poor that stood about him ; yet his bundle or roll of cloth was never less. Then said they, What should this be ? This is, said the shepherds, to shew you that he who has a heart to give of his labor to the poor shall never want wherewithal. He that watereth shall be watered himself. And the cake that the widow gave to the prophet did not cause that she had the less in her barrel."

How apt, too, in this connection, are those beautiful lines by the authoress of *The Schon-berg-Cotta Family :*

" Is thy cruse of comfort failing ? Rise and share it with
      another,
And through all the years of famine, it shall serve thee
      and thy brother :
Love divine will fill thy storehouse, or thy handful still
      renew :
Scanty fare for one will often make a royal feast for two.

" For the heart grows rich in giving ; all its wealth is
      living grain ;
Seeds which mildew in the garner, scattered, fill with gold
      the plain.
Is thy burden hard and heavy ? Do thy steps drag
      wearily ?
Help to bear thy brother's burden ; God will bear both it
      and thee.

" Numb and weary on the mountains, wouldst thou sleep
    amidst the snow ?
Chafe that frozen form beside thee, and together both
    shall glow.
Art thou stricken in life's battle? Many wounded 'round
    thee moan :
Lavish on their wounds thy balsam, and that balm shall
    heal thine own.

" Is the heart a well left empty? None but God its void can
    fill ;
Nothing but a ceaseless fountain can its ceaseless longings
    still.
Is the heart a living power? Self-entwined, its strength
    sinks low ;
It can only live in loving, and by serving love will grow.

ANDREW FULLER.

CHAPTER VI.

IN LABORS ABUNDANT.

"The profession of the physician has been more successfully than any other secular employment, grafted upon that of a spiritual guide to the heathen."
—WILLIAM R. WILLIAMS.

"The Holy Supper is kept, indeed,
In whatso we share with another's need:
Not what we give, but what we share,—
For the gift without the giver is bare;
Who gives himself with his alms feeds three,—
Himself, his hungering neighbor, and Me."
—LOWELL

The words of a certain biographer regarding the imperfect subject of his sketch have frequently come to mind in the writing of these pages. "It was the fashion of old," says that author, "when an ox was led out for sacrifice to Jupiter, to chalk the dark spots, and give the offering a false show of unblemished whiteness. Let us fling away the chalk," he adds, "and boldly say—the victim *is* spotted, but it is not therefore in vain that his mighty heart is laid on the altar of men's highest hopes."

Like all the rest of us, John Thomas had his defects. He was somewhat fickle, hasty of speech and improvident. He was human. And more human elements would appear in biographies if God had the writing of them all. But we are distinctly taught that "God hath chosen the weak things of the world to confound the things which are mighty"; and that He rules in the earth is the more evident from the fact that the nations are being won to Jesus Christ through the labors of men and women who are feeble and faulty.

To what remains, then, of the defective, but nevertheless fruitful, career of the first Baptist missionary to Bengal let us hold our attention.

So eager were those connected with the East India Company for wealth that they jealously watched against any innovations which they thought might in any way conflict with their commercial designs.* At the very time the newly-chosen missionaries were preparing to depart, the government of Christian England was deciding against efforts to spread the gospel among the Hindoos. The East was not looked upon as a field in which to win triumphs for Christ, but simply a place for gold getting. Therefore, thinking the spread of the gospel would not subserve, but rather hinder, the attainment of their sordid ends, the East India Com-

---

*For a brief account of this Company, and the way the friends of missions had to fight in order to secure in its charter clauses permitting missionaries to go to India and labor there, see the author's monograph on *William Carey*, to be had of the American Baptist Missionary Union, Boston, or of the Baptist Book and Tract Society, Halifax.

pany took an unfriendly attitude toward heralds
of the Cross. The ships then sailing to the East
were owned by this Company, and they would
not permit missionaries to be borne over the
waters in them.

After the farewell meeting at Leicester,
Thomas and Carey, accompanied by the devoted
Pearce, went to London to make arrangements
for the missionaries' departure. Inquiries were
entered into as to the possibilty of obtaining
leave of the Court of Directors for their transit.
Charles Grant, who was one of the directors,
and much unlike most of them, was conferred
with ; and while he would gladly have done
what he could to get Carey off, he would not be
party to the return of his medical associate.
It becoming clear, then, that license for their
going could not be secured, it was decided
boldly to take shipping without it. By some
good people this action was deprecated ; but
Fuller, always to the front, and generally sound
in heart and head, thus made answer : "The
apostles and primitive ministers were commanded to go into all the world and preach the
gospel to every creature ; nor were they to stop
for the permission of any power upon earth ;
but to go and take the consequences. If a man
of God, conscious of having nothing in his heart

unfriendly to any civil government whatever, but determined in all civil matters to obey, and teach obedience to the 'powers that be,' puts his life in his hand, saying, 'I will go, and, if I am persecuted in one city, I will flee to another '—whatever the wisdom of the world may decide upon his conduct, he will assuredly be acquitted, and more than acquitted, at a higher tribunal." Accordingly, arrangements were made with the captain of the *Oxford* to take Carey and his boy Felix, then between seven and eight, and Thomas and wife and their only surviving child, £250 being paid as passage money. But before the hour of sailing, word came to captain White that complaint would be lodged against him if a certain unlicensed passenger, whose name was not given, were allowed to proceed to India. Pursuant to this, Carey and son and Thomas left the ship, £150 being restored, the balance being kept for the conveyance of Mrs. Thomas and child, and " the black boy Andrew," who were going with the Company's permission.

By this event the friends of the infant cause were thrown into perplexity. But day dawned quickly. With brief delay passage was secured on board a Danish Indiaman, Mrs. Carey coming meanwhile into fitness and willingness to accom-

pany her husband, and on the 13th of June,
1793, twenty-one days after the *Oxford* left, the
Kron Princessa Maria, took Thomas and Carey
from the much-loved shores they were never to
see again. The Reign of Terror in France, be
it observed, was at this time at its height.

On the 11th of November following, Calcutta
was reached—Thomas during the voyage having
been a faithful teacher and Carey an apt pupil
of the Bengali language. As they passed up
the Bay of Bengal they met a ship which was
bearing away the retiring Governor-General of
India, Lord Cornwallis, who had twelve years
before surrendered the British army to General
Washington. At once Carey engaged Ram
Basu, Thomas's former instructor, to lead him
on in acquiring the vernacular. In the way of
provision for temporal necessities the Society
had furnished the brethren £150 worth of goods,
to be disposed of upon reaching destination,
foreign exchanges being then unknown.

It was Carey's plan, as set forth in his
Enquiry, to secure and cultivate a piece of
ground for the payment of current expenses.
With this in mind, he removed to Bandel,
twenty-five miles up the river, a cheap and
quiet place, from which numerous heathen villages were easily accessible. Here he met the

venerable Kiernander, then in his eighty-fourth
year. But the place proved unsuitable for his
purpose, so that in about a month they were
again in Calcutta. Temporarily Thomas re-
sumed medical practice, while Carey looked
about for land. At length the latter found
what he desired at Dehatta, on the borders of
the Soondarbans, a tiger-haunted and malarial
region forty miles south-east of Calcutta, and
turned to Thomas, who had taken charge of the
finances, for the needed money, only to learn
that it had all been spent.

But how could Thomas be expected by this time
to have very much ? To the Committee at home
he had given the lowest possible estimate of living
in places outside of Calcutta; but upon this
amount a family living in Calcutta would starve.
Carey, brought up in the most rigid economy,
and remembering, perhaps, the starvation rates
which Thomas had before mentioned, seems to
have expected that two families, his own con-
sisting of seven members, could live upon £150
for more than two months, and then have left
enough for the purchase of land. Anyway, he
was much surprised when he found that all the
funds had been exhausted, and at the height of
his disappointment wrote the Committee about
the extravagance of his colleague. Thomas,

setting up the practice of medicine, had need of
some show of respectability beyond that of his
brother, and inasmuch as his family was smaller
than Carey's, there was due him something
which could properly be used for this purpose.
The complaints which Carey sent home regarding Thomas at this time have had wide circulation ; but scant currency has been given to
what he wrote after a fuller view had been had
of the case. He came to say, and to say it as
a matter of justice and not of generosity merely,
that he wished all he had then written to the
disadvantage of Thomas were " forever sup-
pressed and buried in oblivion." Thomas, as
everybody knows, was not a good financier; and
no one would attempt to exonerate him in all
his mismanagement. But there is enough
which may fairly be laid to his charge without
running over into exaggeration.

But Carey went, nevertheless, to Dehatta,
having borrowed money, and was there kindly
received (Feb. 6, 1794) and temporarily provided for at the home of Charles Short, afterwards the husband of Mrs. Carey's sister. A
few acres of land were here procured, and a
hut was built ; but soon the family was much
afflicted by sickness,—Carey's own troubles
being greatly augmented the while by the up-

braidings of his wife, who never shared in her husband's missionary aspirations. At the same time prosperity was not attending Thomas in Calcutta ; and the young enterprise of rooting Christianity in that dark land seemed doomed to death. But God had not deserted His servants. And it was through John Thomas, mark you, that William Carey was brought out of his present dire distress.

On the evening of January 3rd, 1794, a heavy affliction came to the Udny family. Robert Udny and wife were drowned by the upsetting of a boat off Calcutta. The mother was then with her son George at Malda, and to the afflicted ones there Thomas straightway wrote an affectionate letter of condolence. Then there came to him in return an urgent invitation to visit Malda, an invitation accepted to the great comfort of the sorrowful. One day while out riding, Mrs. Udny said : "You have no mind, Doctor, for indigo works, have you?" "Yes, madam," he replied, "I should like it very much, if any one would so employ me." Just then Mr. Udny was erecting two factories, one at Moypaldiggy and the other at Mudnabatty, twenty miles apart ; and not only was Thomas engaged to take charge of the former, but he put in a plea on Carey's behalf and

secured for him the latter, the returns for
their services being partly dependent upon the
measure of their success. In connection with
the pursuit, there was much leisure from November to June, so that ample opportunities were
afforded for study and preaching. At this
change of circumstances the missionaries wrote
to England relieving the Society for the present
of any financial burden on their account, and
suggesting that other needy fields be looked to.
But Carey and Thomas were none the less
bound to the organization under which they had
been sent out.

The gain of this to the mission just at this
stage it would be difficult to estimate. The
Society could as yet help them but little anyway, and secular employment of some sort
these men must be engaged in or the East India
Company would not permit them to remain
within British jurisdiction. Then later when
Carey has acquired Bengali, and the time is ripe
for entering more fully into distinctively missionary service, a welcome is found within
Danish dominions at Serampore, where the work
marches on with rapid strides.

On the first day of November, 1795, Samuel
Powell, who had gone to India upon the same
ship with Mrs. Thomas, was baptized by Carey ;

after which Carey, Powell, Thomas and Long, whom Thomas baptized, organized themselves into a Christian Church—the first Baptist Church in India. Writing his father about this date Thomas said : " I act part of the day as a servant, part as a master, doctor, missionary, merchant, justice of the peace, and can even make bread occasionally. I like the part of a strolling missionary best of all ; and, next to that, it is a pleasure to heal the poor and relieve them from any of their pains and diseases. I have patients from all parts, all poor and costly, but some of my sweetest moments are spent in giving them relief."

In indigo culture neither of the brethren succeeded, not because of inefficiency or lack of care, but chiefly on account of the heavy rains, and to some extent because they did not have committed to them such discretionary power in the conduct of affairs as was needful for best results. Near the close of 1797 Thomas resigned his position, thinking Udny would soon, owing to former failures, abandon the indigo works. In some respects his stay at Moypaldiggy was the happiest portion of his life. With him he had his family, from whom he had long been separated; and near by was Carey, with whom he prayed and planned and held sweet converse. And he was now, too, the servant of an honorable missionary Society. Had he continued longer here it seems as though it would have been better for him ; for a period ensues in which he has no certain resting place. In 1798, not to go into wearisome detail, he itinerated in much poverty. At Cooleadean, in 1799, he rented an indigo factory for himself, but met with utter failure. Then he turned to the sugar business and made no improvement. And then at Supur he passed through an alarming illness.

In 1799, the year of George Washington's death, Carey's work ceased in connection with the factory at Mudnabatty ; and he and Fountain, who had joined him in 1796, proposed erecting buildings for missionary purposes at Kidderpore, twelve miles from Mudnabatty, where there was a small out-factory. Carey cherished the idea of a number of missionary families uniting in a Community, somewhat after the Moravian model. But the East India Company would not allow him to carry out his designs within its territory, and therefore they proceeded to the Danish settlement of Serampore, on the west bank of the Hoogli, fourteen miles from Calcutta, reaching there January 10th, 1800. A few months before this, William

Ward, Joshua Marshman and wife, Daniel
Brunsdon and wife, William Grant and wife,
and Miss Tidd, afterwards the wife of Fountain
and then of Ward, had come to strengthen the
mission. A Danish ship took the first English
missionaries to the Hindoos, and an American
ship took reinforcements. The refusal of the
East India Company to carry messengers of the
Cross to India in their vessels was overruled to
the glory of God by the gainful contact which
Baptist Churches of the United States had with
some of these outgoing heralds.*

Thomas, now in the Birbhum district, wished
that one or more of the new missionaries would
join him ; but they did not go to the East with
flattering impressions concerning him. Fuller's
conversation with Charles Grant had not turned
to Thomas's advantage ; and the effect of Carey's
early letters had not been nullified. Therefore
the recent comers did not care to enter into
closest relations with him.

But now and again Thomas turned from his
evangelizing tours to visit the toilers at Serampore. By this time he had assumed the Bengali
dress, that he might get about the more easily
and economically. On the 26th of November,

---

*See *Serampore Letters*, (1800-1816,) by Leighton and
Mornay Williams.

1800, he set the broken arm of a Hindoo, Krishna Pal by name, and afterwards preached to him the plain gospel in a very effective manner. The man had heard the message before this, but not savingly. "When his arm was set right," says Thomas, "he complained still of pain, but more of himself, as a sinner ; and with many tears, cried out : ' I am a great sinner ! A great sinner am I ! Save me, Sahib ! save me !' Then with unusual light and enlargement of soul, I renounced all power to save him myself, and referred him to Jesus, *my* Saviour, of whose mission and power to save all those who come unto God by Him I spoke many things." The result was, Krishna was converted ; and, upon the last Lord's Day of 1800, was baptized by Carey in t'e river Ganges. Henceforth he was an earnest gospel preacher among his own countrymen for more than twenty years ; and his hymn, translated by Dr. Marshman, beginning :

"O thou, my soul, forget no more
The Friend who all thy sorrows bore,"

is now widely sung in Christian and in heathen lands. But poor Thomas was not permitted to witness the baptism of the first convert made by the mission—the baptism of the one he had been instrumental in leading to Jesus.

CHAPTER VII.

DERANGEMENT AND DEATH.

"That man is very strong and powerful who has no more hopes for himself, who looks not to be loved any more, to be admired any more, to have any more honour or dignity, and who cares not for gratitude; but whose sole thought is for others, and who only lives on for them."—HELPS.

"I rejoice that the broken barque shall come to land, and that Christ will on the shore welcome the sea-sick passenger."—SAMUEL RUTHERFORD.

Occasionally in the previous career of the subject of this sketch there were suggestions of the possibility of his mind giving way; and around the date of Krishna's immersion came a combination of circumstances which brought the worst to pass. His health was broken and his financial matters were in a distressing state. December 17th, 1800, he entered Serampore, and although greatly wearied with toilsome journeyings, he sat up all night with Brunsdon, who was seriously sick and who had been anxiously looking for the "beloved physician." "This I feel," wrote Thomas, "is my joy, that I should be permitted to be a comfort and service to the body of His saints." Next morning a letter was handed him from Fuller, reproach-

ing him for long-continued silence ; and at once,
without taking sleep, reply was made to this
epistle. The Secretary said that the action in
leaving Moypaldiggy "conveyed an idea of the
mission being only a secondary object with
him." This cut deeply and was not just.
Thomas humbly says in answer to the charge :—
"It may appear so ; but still, if the Society
were to leave me, and every mortal upon the
earth, I, nevertheless, had rather die in the
mission work than live upon the wealth of all
India out of it."

In the afternoon of the same day he crossed
the river and preached to groups of hearers
and at night attended a conference of missionaries. Next morning he was employed in looking for a house that he might live in Serampore.
Then he met a number of visitors, among them
Krishna, whom he longed to see break caste
and follow Christ in baptism. In speaking of
the words he heard the day his arm was set,
Krishna said : "I shall never forget them.
Oh, how they have softened my heart, Sahib ;
but I have confessed my sins ; I have obtained
righteousness of Jesus Christ ; and I am free."
In the afternoon Thomas went to Krishna's
house and there addressed a few listeners.
" What a day this has been ! " he wrote in his

diary. "It is now midnight, but it is still
noon-tide with me."

Other days went by filled up with anxious
watchings over Brunsdon, exciting interviews
with inquiring natives, ardent preaching, con-
ferences with brethren and fervent wrest-
lings at a throne of grace. Then followed
the relinquishment of caste on the part of
Krishna and Gokul. "This blessed day, thrice
blessed day, I praise the most high God,
possessor of heaven and earth, for Gokul and
Krishna have thrown away their caste! Yes-
terday I was so confident that the time was
come, that all my brethren imputed it to my
too sanguine disposition—which also Mr. Grant
complained of. But, O my God, what had my
disposition to do in this matter? Or what my
polluted hand? Or what any arm of flesh?
No hand was here but Thine. Thou alone hast
done it, when some of us least expected it; and
I was not too sanguine in Thee, neither can any
ever be." But amidst this he seems to have
had apprehension of pending calamity to himself
as he adds: "Oh how unutterable is my joy!
But, lest I be exalted above measure, some
terrible messenger is at hand!—Welcome, good
messenger, terror along! for my soul is not
afraid." Then speedily there appeared clear.

evidences of his insanity. In unstudied rhyme his disorded mind ran on in this fashion : " Sing a song of fifteen years,—if, my soul, thou canst for tears. Sing of hope and sing of doubt, sing how all is well made out." He attended the church meeting where Felix Carey, Krishna and Gokul (who drew back for a little) came to relate their experiences, and all the time kept growing worse. On the 28th of December, Carey baptized his own son Felix and Krishna ; but Thomas, who had anticipated the day with so much delight, had to be confined in the school room. But he could hear them sing the hymn,

"Jesus, and sha'l it ever be—
A mortal man ashamed of Thee ?"

which his pandit, Padma Lochan, had put into Bengali. At the same time, Mrs. Carey was likewise insane.

Directly Carey and Marshman took their deranged brother to Calcutta, where he was placed in the hospital for lunatics. In twenty-four days, however, he was fit to be released ; an l accepting an invitation from Ignatius Fernandez, a Eurasian trader, who had been baptized at Serampore on the 18th of January, he set out for Dinajpoor. The journey thither was a sad one, because all along the river, which had been so much traversed by the now feeble man, he

was reminded of the little fruit of his efforts in
the towns and villages where he had long and
earnestly preached Christ. He entered somewhat into the feelings of the Master when He
wept over unbelieving Jerusalem.

It will be seen how poorly Thomas was now
able to shoulder any responsibility. He had had
mental restoration, and was not again insane,
but he was physically wrecked. Yet notwithstanding this he sought, under pressure from
creditors, and from strong desire to owe no man
anything, some way by which to become clear
with the world. So he entered, at the advice
of some acquaintances, upon indigo-culture for
himself at a little out-factory in Sadamahal,
twenty-four miles from Dinajpoor. This move
displeased the Serampore brethren, who thought
it meant deeper indebtedness; but his designs
were laudable, though he did not succeed.
Many mournful days had he had before, but
none were sadder than these he now passed
through. News came to him of Brunsdon's
death; rains fell to the destruction of his
indigo crop; and, worse than all, while trying
to do his best and greatly needing sympathy,
severe criticisms reached him from Serampore.
" Driven from among men, I sit alone, friend-
less, almost comfortless, as to this world, for

weeks together. . . . I have been in doubt and perplexity of soul, such as I never knew before; in darkness, without any light: my bodily strength decayed; my heart literally sore; my spirits drunk up. But I know the light as well as the darkness, the voice of the Shepherd as well as the voice of the wolf. I heard Him say, 'Come unto me.' I know His voice and feel His glorious power also, strengthening vile me unto patience and long-suffering with some joyfulness, giving thanks unto the Father." As the days and nights went, his physical condition grew worse, while he still goaded himself on to work.

But as the end drew nearer, happier experiences began to predominate. More and more did his eyes open to the promises until he could say: "My troubles look like mice before these thunderbolts." Something of the warmth and brightness of his eternal home began to reach his weary spirit. In the following stanzas he found an exact expression of his mind :

"Thou art my Pilot wise;
   My compass is Thy word;
My soul each storm defies,
   While I have such a Lord.
      I trust Thy faithfulness and power,
      To save me in the trying hour.

"Though rocks and quicksands deep
   Through all my passage lie,

Yet Christ will safely keep,
And guide me with His eye.
My anchor, hope, shall firm abide,
And I each boisterous storm outride.

" By faith, I see the land,
The port of endless rest.
My soul, thy sails expand,
And fly to Jesus' breast.
Soon shall I reach that heavenly shore,
Where winds and waves distress no more !"

After the middle of September, he was com-
pelled to leave the solitude of Sadamahal and
go on horseback to Dinajpoor for medical advice and friendly assistance. Part of the journey was made in scorching sun and part in
drenching rain, so that a violent fever ensued.
On the morning of the 29th, he made the last
entry in his journal, indicative of the dying
man's undying devotion : " O Lord, accept my
early thanks through the Redeemer, in whom
Thou art well pleased, and may they never cease
to flow from this heart . . . I conversed
with a Brahman on death, on the shasters, on
idols, and the worship of them, till he made a
sudden bow and disappeared.' A day or two
before the end came, he repeated the first verse
of, "Jesus, lover of my soul," in a manner so
impressive, that new beauties were brought
from it to the listeners. "Unable to read,"
writes his friend Powell, "his mind was so stored
with Scripture that he would often cite passages
appropriate to his situation and circumstances,

from which he derived much comfort. His
soul was continually breathing after God.
Once, while he was in great pain, he cried out
in triumph, 'O death, where is thy sting?' His
last agonies were exceeding great. Several
hours before his death he became speechless, and
continued so, till his soul burst from her prison
and winged its way to a brighter and better
world, where pains and sorrows are unknown.
He expired on the 13th day of October (1801),
and was buried by the side of Mr. Fountain."

Concerning the departed missionary, his
brethren had many kind things to say after he
had gone from them. " Never shall I forget
the time," wrote Ward, "after setting Krishna's
arm, he talked to him with such earnestness
about his soul's salvation that Krishna wept like
a child. Thus brother Thomas led the way to
India, and was the means of the planting of the
church by the conversion of *the first native.*"
Marshman wrote : " When everything is considered, he was a most useful instrument in the
mission. To him it is owing, under God, that
the Hindoos now hear the Word of Life. His
unquenchable desires after their conversion in-
duced him to relinquish his secular employment
on board the *Earl of Oxford* East Indiaman,
to devote himself to that object alone, which

ultimately led our beloved Society to their engagement in the present mission. His peculiar
talents, his intense, though irregular spirituality,
and his constant attachment to that beloved
object, the conversion of the heathen, will
render his memory dear as long as the mission
endures." Carey declared that he was "one
of the most affectionate and close exhorters to
genuine godliness, and to a close walk with God,
that could be thought of."

One cannot but wish, with Mr. Lewis, that
the fragrance of these and other similar utter-
ances had reached him whilst his fainting spirit
might have been sustained thereby. Truly a
fallen world is helped up to God much more by
tender and sympathetic word spoken in the
ear that yet hears than by eulogistic obituary
or epitaph.

Something very touching is related of Mrs.
Robert Burdette, who died a number of years
ago in Burlington, Iowa. She was a great lover of flowers; and during her protracted illness,
beautiful bouquets were continually being
brought her. When nigh unto death, and thinking of the funeral rites, she knew that a profusion
of flowers would be brought to her burial; and
she requested, in the spirit of her Lord, that,
instead of making such use of them, they should

be taken to the poor sick and suffering ones of her city, for to the dead they could not minister, but to the living they might carry something of the joy and light of God. Ah, if we have affectionate words to utter and generous deeds to perform, let them be spoken and done while yet they may be of some avail. Lives greatly complained of because bearing scant fruit, would be much more noble if only friends near by showed larger sympathy and more prayerfully plied the ministry of cheer. Speak out your appreciation now, O reader, and reserve it not to be chiseled in marble. As you tread life's rugged highway, where go many who are foot-sore, it will not be amiss frequently to call up Browning's line :

" A handsome word or two gives help."

Or to remember, and often repeat, those lines by Milton :

"Apt words have power to suage the tumors of a troubled mind,
And are as balm to festered wounds."

CHAPTER VIII.

FINANCIAL DIFFICULTIES.

" That which makes head against the greatest opposition, gives best demonstration that it is strongest."
—BUNYAN'S " Old Honest."

" On the whole, we make too much of faults ; the details
of the business hide the real centre of it. . . . . What
are faults, what are the outward details of a life, if the
inner secret of it, the remorse, temptations, true, often-
baffled, never-ended struggle of it be forgotten ? "
—THOMAS CARLYLE.

Thus hastily have we tried to review, and to
review justly, the career of Dr. John Thomas,
from birth at Fairford to burial at Dinajpoor ;
but before taking our leave of him, let us dwell
more in detail upon a few things which have
already had passing notice.

In the first place let us look at his financial
record. Those who know anything of the man
at all are aware that he was most always
heavily in debt.

Now let none speak of this as though it were
a light thing. The people of God should have
scrupulous care to avoid reproach because of
any unfaithfulness in business transactions.
The gospel is to be borne into the marts of
trade through exceptionally upright dealing.

What care I what you say, remarks Emerson, when what you do stands over my head and thunders in my ears so loud I cannot hear what you say!

But any who follow Thomas's history will observe how many things, over which he had no control whatever, conspired against his financial prosperity. When he was sailing as surgeon, the officers of Indiamen were allowed to take merchandise in their vessels on their own account, and to dispose of it as they might have opportunity. Thomas, availing himself of this privilege, had gains upon his second voyage exceeding £500. Relinquishing the ship for mission work cost him quite a sum, but he thought this would be much more than made good by profits from the Indian products he sent back for the English market. But articles of English manufacture were introduced at home just in time to diminish the demand for what he sent thither. Hence, that which he expected would realize £2,000, brought only £924, and consequently he was thrown into embarrassment from which he never recovered. To the end of his days he was much hampered by this loss. Had the Society relieved him before he came to India as their missionary; or, better, had he found a way of relieving himself,

his subsequent history would certainly have
taken on a brighter hue.

An inquisitive stranger wanted to know of a
Christian shoemaker what was his business.
The reply was : "Pointing lost souls to the Saviour; but I make shoes to pay expenses." The
business of Thomas was the same ; but he had
to keep to some secular calling as a means of
partial support. And in every such calling to
which he turned his hand he met with failure.
Year after year the rains destroyed his indigo
crops; and when he went into the sugar business,
some unlooked-for turn left him in penury. He
went at a good many things, and would sometimes have done better to have been less forward
in seeking change ; but this very haste was
due, in part, to eagerness to mend matters.

His generous disposition, too, made further
havoc of his finances. No man was ever more
ready than he to run and minister to the poor
and the suffering, and upon such he made no
small expenditure. After he was bereft of
support from Charles Grant, and his friends at
Malda settled upon him a monthly allowance,
he made a characteristic entry in his journal,
viz: "Very much enjoyed relieving the Brahman
out of my new salary." Had he been less kind,
he would, perhaps, have been more kindly
remembered.

Then his supposed converts took advantage of him. To help them out of distress, he would sometimes become responsible for them, having confidence that unto him they would prove true. Eager to do anything that would put any into situations where they would be helped in any degree from heathenism to Christianity, he was not always prudent. In short, he was toiling for India when circumstances were decidedly more harassing than they were a little later.

"His compassion to the poor," says Carey, " leads him to give far beyond his ability." Nearly a year after he left Moypaldiggy, Fountain wrote : " Brother T.'s removal is a great loss to this part of the country. I understand he has been thronged with patients from place to place wherever he has gone. Perhaps there never was a person in this country who has done so much in this way for the poor and needy as he has. The blessings of hundreds ready to perish have fallen upon him. His regard for them is so great that I have known him to get no sleep for a whole night when he has had a surgical operation to perform the next day. He has many qualifications which render him the fittest person for a missionary that could anywhere be found." Carey added : " His home is constantly surrounded by the afflicted, and the cures wrought by him would have gained any physician or surgeon in Europe the most extensive reputation." And the rendering of such services cost him outlay of money as well as of time and strength. He himself records (June 17, 1798): "I have hundreds of patients and I go on in my old way. I maintain here and there a most deplorable object, while I am in want myself; but it looks to me like murder to neglect those who are actually ready to perish, on any pretense whatever." Once in writing Fuller, he said: "In England the poor receive the benefits of the gospel, in being fed and clothed by those who know it not, and know not by what they are moved; . . . but here! Oh miserable sight! I have found the pathways stopped up by sick and wounded people, perishing with hunger and distress, and that in a populous neighborhood, where plenty of people pass by, some singing, others talking, but none showing any more compassion than as though they were dying weeds, and not dying men. There is such a blessedness and sweetness in giving, especially to those who have been accustomed to feel distress of their own, that I wonder that all men who are able do not indulge themselves in this pleasure."

Some people can be in debt and have very little concern about it; but Thomas was not one of that sort Most cruel wrong is done him if it is thought that he was indifferent to the claims of creditors. Earnestly did he pray God to help him pay what he owed; and strenuously did he labor in conformity with his petitions. Once when on the very eve of a financial success, and when it seemed certain that an important sum would quickly come to him, he cheerfully penned the words: " It has now pleased the Lord to hear and answer my prayers, old and new, offered up ten years ago and since, that He would remember His words, ' The silver and the gold is mine,' and grant me money to pay my debts, and that I may have to give to him that needeth; that I may render to every man his due, and owe no man anything." But in this, as usual, his hopes were blasted. "No answer to prayer respecting my temporal affairs. Yet I will wait on Him, and wait for Him, and look to Him." Never, never, does this oft-disappointed man charge God foolishly! Dwell thoughtfully upon this, O ye who murmur much under the Divine hand.

CHAPTER IX.

BEGINNINGS OF THE BENGALI BIBLE.

"A sublimer thought cannot be conceived than when a poor cobbler formed the resolution to give to the millions of Hindoos the Bible in their own language."
—WILLIAM WILBERFORCE.

When Thomas had decided to devote himself to missionary work in India he set about at once, and earnestly, acquiring the Bengali tongue. Halhed had, in 1778, printed a Bengali grammar; but there was no Bengali dictionary, nor were there any Bengali books to give assistance. But in Ram Basu he had a clever teacher, and in a comparatively short time, though it meant much more for him to "plod" than for Dr. Carey, he was preaching to the Bengalese.

It was not simply in order to be able to preach to the heathen, however, that he sought to know their language. He longed to see a Bengali Bible in their hands, and he endeavored to do something to give it to them. To Fuller he wrote in the end of 1796: "I would give a million pounds sterling, if I had it, to see a Bengali Bible. O most merciful God, what an in-

WILLIAM CAREY.

estimable blessing will it be to these millions!
Methinks all heaven and hell will be moved at
the Bible's entering such a country as this.
O Lord, send forth Thy light and Thy truth!"

But the people were not entirely kept from
reading anything out of God's Book until a
whole Gospel should be translated and printed.
This man who loved them, as no other one in
India loved them in those earlier days, was
accustomed to write upon slips of paper, in his
own admirable Bengali caligraphy. striking
Scripture texts and then to distribute them
through his hungry audiences. And as the
weeks and months went on he was doing what
he could, amid numerous duties, to prepare
larger portions for the printer. After he had
translated the Gospel of Matthew he sought to
have it put to press, but met with various
hindrances therein. Then he completed the
translation of Mark and the Epistle of James.
During the voyage to England and back, Genesis
was translated, and just after returning to
India he did the Gospel of Luke. One of his
objects in visiting his native land was to make
arrangements for types and presses. Sorely
was his soul tried by the delays in publication,
but greater accuracy of translation was thereby
secured. By July of 1800 the Gospel of Mat-

thew was published, and this was in the main
his own translation. To him there came no
little joy in being able, near the close of his life,
to carry about copies of this for distribution in
his journeyings.

On the 7th of February, 1801, two weeks
after Dr. Thomas's release from the hospital, the
last sheet of the Bengali New Testament was
put into Dr. Carey's hands at Serampore.
" When a volume had been bound, " says Dr.
George Smith, " it was reverently offered to
God by being placed on the Communion table
of the Chapel, and the mission families and
the new-made converts gathered around it with
solemn thanksgiving to God. As Tyndale's
version had broken the yoke of the papacy in
England, Carey thus struck the first deadly
blow at Brahmanism in its stronghold."

But Thomas had a hand, let us remember, in
giving the Bible to the Hindoos. If it was
a thing so sublime for Carey to conceive and
execute so much in the matter of Scripture translation, what Thomas hoped and prayed for, and
what he in a small measure achieved, is not
altogether unworthy of mention. "The small-
est thing." says John Foster, " rises into
consequence when regarded as the commence-
ment of what has advanced, or is advancing,
into magnificence."

CHAPTER X.

" What is the meaning of the Christian life?
Is it success? or vulgar wealth, or name?
Is it a weary struggle—a mean strife
For rank, low gains, ambition, or for fame?
What sow we for? The world? For fleeting time?
Or far-off harvests, richer, more sublime?
The brightest life on earth was one of loss,
The noblest head was wreathed with sharpest thorn,
Has He not consecrated pain—the Cross?
What higher crown can Christian's brow adorn?
Be we content to follow on the road
Which men count failure, but which leads to God."

Indigo culture was no more Thomas's business than tent-making was Paul's. It was the ruling purpose of his life to direct the lost to the world's only Saviour. As a preacher of the gospel to the heathen he had remarkable power, as abundant evidence goes to show. His addresses were full of life, and very tender, so that he was gladly heard by the common people. On the 27th of February, 1788, the year Judson was born, he preached his first sermon in Bengali.

It was with wonderful tact and ability that he met and overcame the objections and opposition of the natives. Once when on a journey he saw a multitude congregating for worship of one of the heathen gods. Coming up and making his way through the company, he took an elevation near the idol, the onlooking people wondering, as he did so, what the European could be about. Beckoning for silence, and pointing to the image, he said : " It has eyes" (then turning to the assembly), " but it cannot see ! It has ears,—but it cannot hear! It has a nose,—but it cannot smell ! It has hands, —but it cannot handle ! It has a mouth,—but it cannot speak ! Neither is their any breath in it ! " An old man who was present, struck by what was so evident, cried out : " It has feet, —but it cannot run away !" And then a universal shout arose and the faces of the priests were covered with shame.

No matter what secular employment he was obliged to engage in, nor how many and wearing were other claims upon him, he found much space for preaching. " He was well understood wherever he went," says his sympathetic biographer, "and he so spoke in Bengali, that crowds everywhere delighted to listen to his addresses, and were often deeply moved by his pungent and affectionate appeals. In dealing with those subtle and difficult metaphysical questions which the learned or unlearned Hindoo is ever ready to propound and

discuss, and which are so well adapted to blunt
the edge and turn the point of ordinary exhor-
tation, he showed great ability and power.
Those questions, in their Bengali aspects, he
was perhaps the first to encounter as a Christian
evangelist; and the ingenuity, practical good
sense, and profound reverence for the divine
honor which his arguments displayed, are
worthy of all admiration by his successors.
He seems to have been singularly fitted to
announce the gospel to the Hindoos, ‘speaking
to them by many similitudes, such as they themselves use,’ ‘who never argue long without a
quotation or a comparison.’ ”

To press on when fruit of effort keeps issuing
to view is comparatively easy; but Dr. Thomas
held to his post amidst direst discouragements.
Indeed we do not every day encounter men
with such unyielding faith in the ultimate triumph of the Cross as he had. If he did not
swiftly see come to pass what he longed for,
he would not on that account lie idly by and
give way to complaint. He loved Jesus, and
he loved the souls of those for whom Jesus
died. He did not belong to the ranks of
weaklings who run from duty at the approach
of harsh criticism and censure. He was in the
employ of God, and to his Employer he strove

to be true to the last.   Just think of the
disappointments which overtook him in his
ministry of love!   In 1788 he was cheered by
the promise of conversion given by his moonshee, Ram Basu.   He remembered that David
Brainerd had joy among North American
Indians at beholding his interpreter accept
Jesus ; and he hoped the same would be done
by his teacher.   But Ram Basu was the first
of many who promised well and turned out ill.
Mohan Chand, the Brahman, disappointed him.
These two he once took to Calcutta that those who
had come to be not altogether friendly to him
there, might behold some fruits of his exertions.
But both remained to the close unwilling to
renounce caste and be baptized.   Then in one
named Parbati, a high-caste man, great hopes
were centred.   From Ram Basu and Parbati,
Thomas took home to Dr. Stennett a letter
appealing for missionaries to their country and
for the whole Bible in their own language.
And to these two, and Mohan Chand also,
letters were sent back from the brethren in
England.   But all three were soon guilty of
gross departures from rectitude, much to the
sorrow of him who yearned over them.   Then
Padma Lochan, Thomas's teacher of Sanscrit,
whose translation of Joseph Grigg's hymn was

sung at Krishna's baptism, gave evidences of inward renewal ; but later on there were lacking satisfactory signs of anything beyond a surface movement.

From time to time other inquirers arose and new felicity came to the heart of him who bore to them the glad tidings. But in-every case until Krishna, the preacher's high expectations were brought to the ground. And who wonders that he wrote one day : " I am quite weary of hearing and seeing hopeful beginnings end in a hopeless manner, or near it. Yardi, like all the rest, is going ; and if ever I meet with any that distinguish themselves by inquiry, attention and seriousness, they only give me pain, where once I felt only pleasure." He elsewhere says : " Sometimes I am not humble, nor lowly, nor meek enough to go without such thoughts as these,—Why should I preach any more, or wait any longer ? Why not go to England and sell holy ballads for my bread, rather than live in these suburbs of hell, where religion itself is as cold as death, and where Satan's seat is, visibly ? Why not go and feed with the flock of Christ in my native country, and give this work up as one which the Lord will not prosper ? I suppose there is a good deal of flesh and blood at the bottom of

all this. But again, I think of my adorable
Master, and some of His servants, like Jeremiah,
and, at a very humble distance, I follow on,
determined at all events to pray and preach
among them here, till I die myself. That cannot now be very long hence, for I am forty-one
years of age, and I feel myself begin to change,
and to lose my health, natural spirits and
strength. I would therefore have you look out
in time for another man to take my place ;—
but do not let him be such an one as I am !
But now I am forgetting the Lord of the vine-
yard. He will send by whom He will send ;
—sometimes by an angel and sometimes by an
ass !"

To those looking only at that which is outward
it would seem that the lot of this man was wholly
miserable. Yet it was not so. Hear the way
he expresses himself in one place, quite remind-
ing us of the seraphic Samuel Rutherford :

" I have preached many a time among the
Hindoos unsuccessfully ; whilst at the same time
I have enjoyed such enlarged views of the solemn
truths I delivered, however undervalued by
them, such liberty in expressing them, and
such a clear, sweet, soul-satisfying taste of the
goodness of God, and of the baseness of every
other independent enjoyment, if there be an

independent enjoyment, as did put it out of all
doubt that Jesus Christ had fulfilled His word
to me, ' Lo, I am with you alway.' . . . I
know what the delicacies of life are, for I have
tasted them. I know what it is to live in ' the
glory of all lands,' and under the best of govern-
ments, as I think. I know what social enjoyments
are ; and I know what it is to enjoy myself, as
the world calls it. And now, could I multiply
all that I know a thousand times, it would be
refuse to me in comparison of that joy, that
new life, that tenfold satisfaction, that inex-
pressible everything, which the presence of
Christ affords. In a hot and wearisome
climate ; surrounded by various things unpleas-
ant to flesh and blood ; absent from all the
churches ; from all my friends and relations,
banished for ever——- No, no ! All is here.
This barren climate is a paradise,—this fiery
atmosphere is cool and refreshing,—all the
churches and all my friends are here, when
Jesus Christ is with me "

But may we not say that the man was
building far better than he knew ? Foundation
laying makes little show. It is exceedingly
difficult to effect any break whatever in a false
religion milleniums old. And who would
assert that of all those who gave Thomas much

pain after much hope, not one had passed from death unto life? Of this we may be confident that the bountiful harvests of later days had connection with his ploughing and sowing in tearful solitude.

It can be affirmed with emphasis that he had strong faith in Him who issued the Great Commission. Writing his father he says (1790): "Of your son's success, he can say very little at present. Sometimes an inquirer starts up; and sometimes two or three together vanish away, to the grief of his very soul; but [and how truthfully he here speaks!] this is a work that requires a broad bottom, and a length of time *to begin* to begin. 'All that the Father giveth me shall come to me'; and whether these dry bones can live, the Lord knows. I believe I must needs go and call them, and say, 'Stand up!'"

Some sympathy was felt for him, and expressed, in his dissapointments, but he replies, mentioning two in whom he has hopes, and adding that several have cheered Carey's heart: "*But if all these should fail, and as many more, we shall then begin again, 'knowing,'* what we cannot prove, perhaps, '*that our labor is not in vain in the Lord.*'"

"Whoever sees, 'neath winter's fields and snow,
The silent harvest of the future good,
God's power must know."

In March of the year he went to rest and reward, he writes as follows : "You ask, ' *What success?*' I know of no question so difficult to answer with precision, just now. Some say, 'None at all'; others say, 'The time is not come'; some say, 'We never shall have any'; others laugh at our labors altogether, and pity the Society at home. We know of ourselves that ' Except the Lord build the house, they labor in vain that build it'; except the Lord remove all the impediments, lay down all the plan, and find all the materials, we labor in vain. Is a foundation to be laid ? Alas, in this work, here is a Mount Vesuvius in every heart to be taken away ! We have labored on the rubbish, and the materials being now in sight, we begin to think little of what our neighbors say; even though Sanballat, the Horonite, and Tobiah, the Ammonite, themselves were here. For our Master-builder is too wise to send all these materials, at the cost of so much blood and treasure, without any design to build.—' *What success?*' Some of the rubbish is taken away; the foundation is prepared ; the Word of Life is translated ; part of it is printed and daily distributing ; many of

the natives are eager to read it; the holy
unction appears on all the missionaries, more
especially of late ; times of refreshing from the
presence of the Lord are solemn, frequent and
lasting.—' *What success?*' I cannot tell; for
some say all this is nothing, and we have been
too ready to join them. But the Builder sends,
and encourages us to go on, and now we have
'a mind to work.' Six persons have been
baptized, four of whom are natives.—' *What
success?*' Who can tell, when only one little
grain, like a mustard seed, is sprung up ? Here
is a door of faith opened, which no man
shutteth. Who can tell of what divinely pene-
trating degree this leaven is, and how far it
reaches, even now ? Multitudes are moving,
bone to bone ! Glory be unto the most high
God, Possessor of heaven and earth ! Amen.
Let all the people say, Amen. Let all the
angels in heaven say, Amen. And let Christ,
the All in all, say, Amen !"

There is a great deal in this connection that
it is hard to pass by without quoting, but we
will detain the reader only a moment more.
Carefully ponder the following words, and mark
well the devotion to God that they evince.
The entire passage from which they are taken
is a remarkable one. " If an angel were to

come and ask me where I wish to be, I would say, ' Where I am.' If he asked me what I wish to be, I would say, ' A faithful witness of Christ amongst the Hindoos, till death.' If he were to ask me what corruption I wished to have vanquished, or what grace I wished enlarged, I would say, ' I wish to know more of Christ ; for that will slay all my corruptions at once, and invigorate and replenish the new man at all points.' And my situation amongst the heathen sometimes seems to make Christ appear more precious, as the want of a Christ amongst them renders their condition more and more inexpressibly deplorable."

As earthly props were cut away, he the more leaned over upon his God, as God designs that men should ever do. Among the latest of his entries, this one is found : "To-day I perceive more friendship and comfort and relief in these three words ' I change not,' than all my friends could give me if they were ever so kind,—more than all the world is worth if it was laid at my feet this moment."

It was a deep desire of his heart that was gratified when he saw Krishna, for many years afterwards an eloquent evangelist, boldly coming forward and professing Christ. But how small was this outcome of his prolonged toil when compared with the anticipations begotten of the study of Isaiah xlix! And yet for the little he was profoundly grateful, his heart once finding expression in the words : "Oh what blessedness to gather in, if it were but one single stalk of the first fruits of that great harvest, the seed of which has been so long and so surely sown in promises, in prophecies, in tokens, and in stirrings of hope in the Church. *Our children, I trust, will live to see many churches of Christ among the heathen.*"

And lo ! how largely has been fulfilled the long-cherished hope of sainted John Thomas, pioneer preacher to benighted Bengalese !

> " The blank interstices
> Men take for ruins, He will build into
> With pillared marbles rare, or knit across
> With generous arches, till the fane's complete."
>
> —E. B. BROWNING.

THE END.

www.ingramcontent.com/pod-product-compliance
Lightning Source LLC
Chambersburg PA
CBHW032158010726
47493CB00008BA/2742